Wish Upon a Gift

It's a wish come true! Read all the books in the Lucky Stars series:

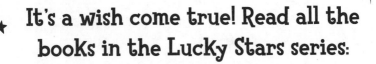

Wish Upon a Gift

by Phoebe Bright
illustrated by Karen Donnelly

SCHOLASTIC INC.

With special thanks to Maria Faulkner

With thanks to all the magical people in my
life for their belief in me

ISBN 978-0-545-42003-7

12 11 10 9 8 7 6 5 4 3 2 1   12 13 14 15 16/0

Printed in China   68
First Scholastic printing, December 2012

Lucky Star that shines so bright,
Who will need your help tonight?
Light up the sky, and thanks to you
Wishes really do come true. . . .

Hello, friend!

I'm Stella Starkeeper, and I want to tell you a secret. Have you ever gazed up at the stars and thought that they could be full of magic? Well, you're right. Stars really are magical!

Their precious starlight allows me to fly down from the sky. I'm always on the lookout for boys and girls who are especially kind and helpful. I train them to become Lucky Stars—people who can make wishes come true!

So the next time you're under the twinkling night sky, look out for me. I'll be floating among the stars somewhere.

Give me a wave!

Love,

Stella Starkeeper

1
Crystal Gifts

Cassie looked at her friend Alex's suitcase and frowned. It was overflowing with beach toys, shells, and brightly colored rocks. Alex picked up his microscope and tried to squeeze it in.

"It won't fit," he groaned.

"Here's one more thing for you to pack," Cassie said.

She held out a photo album with *Alex's Vacation* written on the front. For the last two weeks, Alex and his family had been staying at Starwatcher Towers, the bed-and-breakfast run by Cassie's parents. But now his vacation was over.

"The album's full of good memories," she said, trying to smile.

Alex nodded and cleared his throat. He smiled back, but Cassie could tell he was sad. Even Comet, his little white puppy, had his ears down.

Alex opened the photo album, and Cassie pointed to one of the pictures.

"That's the view from Dad's observatory," she said. "You can see all of Astral-on-Sea from there."

Cassie's dad was an astronomer. At night, he watched the stars from his observatory.

During the day, the observatory had a
spectacular view of the town and the seaside.

Alex flipped the page and laughed. There
was a picture of Comet chasing a ball with
Twinkle, Cassie's old cat.

"They're such good friends," Cassie said.

"Just like us," Alex replied. "I wished for a friend—and you became my best friend ever!"

"Your wish was the first one I helped come true," Cassie said, grinning. "And you're the only person who knows about my magic charms."

4

They both looked down at Cassie's pretty charm bracelet. Every time she granted someone's wish, she received another charm. So far, she had six charms that each gave her a magical power! The bird gave her the power to fly, the crescent moon allowed her to talk to animals, the butterfly let her stop time, the flower made things appear, and the cupcake charm gave her the power of invisibility. *I still need to find out what power my new heart charm gives me, though*, Cassie thought.

"You only need one more charm

now," said Alex. "Then you'll be a Lucky Star, and you can make wishes come true anytime you want!"

Cassie sighed. "If only you could stay and help me."

She blinked away a tear. She couldn't imagine waking up tomorrow and not seeing Alex.

"Thanks for the photo album," Alex said quietly.

"You're welcome," Cassie whispered.

Just then, Alex's mom popped her head around the bedroom door. She noticed the overflowing suitcase right away. "I don't think you'll be able to fit anything else in there, Alex," she said. "Why don't I pack your microscope in my bag?"

Alex nodded, then showed his mom the photo album.

"That's so nice," his mom said, turning the pages. "Should I pack this for you, too?"

"No thanks, I'll carry it on my lap in the car," Alex answered.

"Well, we don't need to leave until tonight, so you have the rest of the day here," his mom said, smiling at them. She took the microscope as she left the room.

"Maybe I can help you earn your last charm today," Alex said to Cassie.

"That would be amazing!" Cassie replied.

Alex danced from foot to foot. "I have something for you, too," he said shyly. He

★ ✳ ★ ✳

lifted a box marked *Top Secret* from the wardrobe.

Cassie opened it. Inside were test tubes filled with beautiful crystals. They twinkled in shades of green, orange, violet, and red.

"Oh, Alex, they look like stars!" she exclaimed.

"I grew the crystals myself," Alex said with a grin.

"Thank you so much," said Cassie. "I'll go and put them in a special place in my room. When you're done packing, we'll do something extra-fun to celebrate your last day here."

Carefully, Cassie carried the crystals to her bedroom. She gave Alex's gift a place of honor on the bookshelf next to her other very favorite things. The crystals looked perfect in her room with its pretty glass ceiling, moon-shaped lamp, and starry wallpaper.

Suddenly, the crystals lit up, shimmering like a rainbow before her eyes! Cassie looked up. High in the blue sky, zooming between the soft, white clouds, a familiar orb of light was heading straight toward her room.

Cassie rushed to pull down the lever on her bedroom wall, and one of the glass panels in her ceiling swung open. Just in time! The orb spun in through the gap and landed with an explosion of starlight.

With a *whizz* and a *fizz* and a *zip-zip-zip*, the light transformed into Stella Starkeeper! Her silver dress shimmered above her glittery leggings and shiny boots.

Cassie gave her friend a big hug. Stella was the one who had given her the charm bracelet for her birthday two weeks ago! Now the little charms tinkled quietly on Cassie's wrist.

"You only need to help make one more wish come true, and then you'll be a Lucky

Star," Stella said, hugging Cassie tightly. "And when you succeed, you won't have to wait for someone to make a wish—you can grant wishes whenever you like."

"Do you think I can do it?" Cassie asked.

Stella's velvety blue eyes sparkled. "I believe in you. Remember, I chose you because you like helping people and making them happy."

Cassie gave a little twirl.

Stella smiled. "But first, you need to prove that you're ready by earning all of the charms," she said.

Cassie nodded.

"I can't wait to be a Lucky Star," she said, sighing. "But I'm so sad that Alex is leaving. Look, he gave me these pretty crystals."

"They're beautiful," Stella said. Then she winked. "Maybe my next clue will cheer you up." She touched the little heart-shaped charm on Cassie's bracelet, making it glow. "The clue to the power of this charm is: *Memories are precious*."

Cassie felt a warm glow in her heart.

"And I've got a special surprise for you," Stella added. "When you become a Lucky Star, I will grant three wishes you can use just for yourself."

Cassie's eyes widened. What a wonderful gift!

Sparkles swirled around Stella. "Don't forget, Cassie," she said. "Memories are precious. . . ."

And then she was gone, leaving Cassie wondering what the clue meant.

2
The Forgetful Ballerina

Tip-tap, swoosh!

The strange noise echoed down the hallway. Cassie peeked out her bedroom door.

Tip-tap, swoosh!

There it was again. It seemed like the sound was coming from her dad's observatory.

Cassie ran to Alex's room.

"Alex!" she called softly.

"I'm just making sure that I've packed everything," he said, opening the door.

"Listen," said Cassie. "Do you hear a strange noise coming from my dad's observatory?"

Alex listened. "I deduce that there's someone up there," he said after a moment. "But I don't think it's your dad."

Quietly, they creeped up the stairs to the observatory and peered through the half-open door. Under the huge domed roof, they saw a girl about their age, dancing around the shiny telescopes. Her lips were curved into a soft smile and her long, dark hair whirled out behind her.

"Who's that?" Alex whispered.

"Izzy Nichols," Cassie replied. "One of the

new guests." Cassie had met her earlier that morning.

Enchanted, they watched Izzy spin around on pointed toes. When she danced, her dress billowed like a colorful cloud. She didn't see Cassie and Alex watching until they burst into applause as she did a perfect pirouette.

Izzy blushed and gave a little curtsy.

"You're amazing," Cassie said.

"Thanks," Izzy replied. "But I have to practice a lot. Our summer school is putting on a show when I get back, and I'm Cinderella."

Holding on to the back of an old leather chair, Izzy turned both feet out and bent her knees, dipping elegantly down and up.

"You make that look so easy," Cassie said.

"These bends are called pliés. They took me a long time to learn," Izzy replied. "I need to learn the steps in the right order, and do them all in time to the music. Like this."

Cassie and Alex watched Izzy run across

the room on her tiptoes, bend, run, leap, and then stop.

"No, that's all wrong," Izzy said with a frown. "Is it a plié first, or a leap? I can't remember. Oh, the show's going to be a disaster!"

Poor Izzy, Cassie thought. *I wonder if my heart charm could help her.*

Just then, Izzy's mom came in. "There you are, Izzy," she said. "Hello, Cassie."

"Hi," Cassie replied with a smile. She'd met Mrs. Nichols earlier, too. "This is Alex. We've been watching Izzy dance — she's fantastic!"

"She's very dedicated, just like a scientist," Alex added.

"She practices every day at home," said Mrs. Nichols. "But we're on vacation now, sweetheart," she told Izzy. "You can relax."

Izzy shook her head. "I'm just so worried about getting the steps wrong for *Cinderella*," she said. "I can't relax." Her eyes filled with tears.

Cassie felt a lump in her own throat. Alex was leaving, and Izzy was unhappy. What a sad day!

Mrs. Nichols gently wiped her daughter's

eyes with a tissue. "I thought you might be worried," she said, "so I found a summer ballet class in Astral-on-Sea. It's a class for everyone, fro beginners to  experienced dancers. It should be fun."

"I guess," said Izzy.

"It starts soon, so if you get changed, I'll drive you there," said Mrs. Nichols with a kind smile. Then she disappeared down the stairs.

Izzy twisted the hem of her dress between her hands. "There will be lots of people at the class who I don't know," she said quietly. "That always makes me extra-nervous and forgetful. Oh, I wish I could remember my ballet routines!"

Cassie and Alex shared a secret smile. Izzy had made a wish.

She's the final person I have to help! Cassie thought, looking at her little heart charm, which was dangling from her bracelet and spinning like a dancer. *But how?*

Izzy was still frowning. Cassie whispered an idea to Alex, who smiled and nodded. Cassie

turned to Izzy and suggested, "What if Alex and I come to the ballet class, too? Then you won't be on your own."

"You would be less nervous," Alex added. "And it's a scientific fact that confidence helps you concentrate."

"Oh, yes! That's really nice of you," Izzy replied, her face lighting up. They all clattered down the stairs. Izzy rushed to her guest room, while Alex followed Cassie to her bedroom.

"Um, I just thought of another scientific fact," Alex said to Cassie. "I have two left feet! I'm not sure how good I'll be in a ballet class."

Poor Alex, Cassie thought. *It's the last day of his vacation, and I know a ballet class isn't exactly his idea of fun. But I need his help!*

Cassie remembered their adventure with Jacey Day, a singer who had stayed at Starwatcher Towers. "You were great as Jacey's backup singer, even though you didn't think you would be," she told Alex. "The dance steps you made up were fantastic!"

"That was fun," Alex admitted. "And I want to help Izzy — and help you earn your last charm. Okay," he agreed, smiling. "I can't let my best friend down."

Cassie gave him a big hug.

Just then, they heard a terrible screech from outside.

"YOWL! MEOW! YOWL!"

Startled, Cassie and Alex looked at each other.

"Twinkle!" they both cried.

"Oh, no," Cassie said as they ran down the stairs. "I wonder what's wrong!"

3

Twinkle's Blanket

Cassie and Alex followed the sound of Twinkle's cries to the side yard, near the driveway.

"YOWL! MEOW! YOWL!"

"Aw, come on," Jamie the garbageman was saying to Cassie's cat. "I can't have you ripping these bags open!"

Twinkle leaped on the garbage bag that Jamie was trying to put in the back of his truck, holding on tight with his claws.

"I'm so sorry," said Cassie, running over.

"That's okay, Cassie," Jamie replied. "I've never seen him like this! It's like he doesn't want me to take the garbage."

"Stop getting in Jamie's way, Twinkle," Cassie said, scooping up her grumpy cat. She turned back to Jamie. "I'll take him inside so you can finish."

"Thanks," Jamie said. "I hope he's okay."

So do I, Cassie thought. *I'll have to ask Twinkle what's wrong.*

Back in the kitchen, Cassie thought hard about her crescent moon charm, which gave her the power to  talk to animals. Silver sparkles swirled around her bracelet, and then over Twinkle and Comet, who trotted along behind Alex.

"Oh, Twinkle. Why are you so

upset?" she asked, stroking his head.

But Twinkle just yowled.

"Please tell me what's wrong," Cassie said, hugging him as they walked into the hallway.

Cassie's mom popped her head around the dining-room door, where she was cleaning up the breakfast dishes.

"I think I know what's up with him," she said, pointing to the fluffy towel under the radiator where Twinkle's blanket used to be. "I had to throw that horrible blanket of his away," she explained, wrinkling her nose. "I could smell it even after I'd washed it!"

Once Cassie's mom had gone back into the dining room, Twinkle yowled, "I loved my blanket!"

"I love this nice towel," Comet yipped, sitting happily in the middle of the cozy new towel.

Twinkle leaped out of Cassie's arms, heading for the back door.

"Quick!" Cassie said to Alex. "We have to follow Twinkle!"

They hurried outside. Twinkle was running toward the orchard.

"He's going too fast for us to catch up with him," said Alex with a groan.

But Cassie had an idea. She grabbed Alex's hand and thought hard about her bird charm. Her wrist tingled as the bracelet's magic began to work, and her feet lifted off the ground. Together, they flew after Twinkle, Comet running along behind.

At the edge of the orchard was a wooden

shed. Twinkle scrambled through a hole in the side. Cassie guided Alex back to the ground, then pressed her nose against the shed window. Inside, she could see a grumpy Twinkle curled up on a pile of old sacks.

She tapped gently on the glass. "Please come out, Twinkle," she said.

"No," Twinkle muttered. "I don't feel wanted anymore."

Cassie looked pleadingly at Alex. "I don't know how to cheer him up."

Alex held his puppy up to the window. "Comet wants to play with you!" he called.

Comet wagged his tail and barked, "Come and chase leaves with me, Twinkle!"

But Twinkle just meowed sadly. "Cats don't have many things of their own," he grumbled. "My blanket was my favorite thing and now it's gone forever. So I'm staying in the shed!"

"Oh, Twinkle," Cassie said. "Mom didn't

mean to upset you. Won't you get hungry in there?"

Twinkle laid his head on his paws. "I'll never be hungry again," he sniffed.

Alex put his arm around Cassie's shoulders. "I know it's hard to leave Twinkle like this," he said, "but we have a ballet class to get to. So put your best left foot forward!"

Alex's joke made Cassie smile. She blew Twinkle a loving kiss through the window.

"I'm going to help Izzy," she told him. "Then I'll come back and help you."

Back at the B&B, they found Cassie's

dad in the kitchen, polishing the lens of one of his telescopes. He was listening to the weather forecast. *"It will be a sunny afternoon, followed by a cloudy night sky,"* the radio announcer was saying.

"Oh, no," Cassie's dad said.

"What's wrong, Dad?" Cassie asked.

"There's going to be an amazing meteor shower tonight," he explained. "I thought Mom and I could watch it to celebrate our wedding anniversary. But it will be too cloudy to see anything in the sky!" With a sigh, he dropped the dusting cloth onto the table.

Cassie gave her dad a hug. What a mess!

So many things are going wrong today, she thought. *But even if nothing else goes right, I'm going to make sure Izzy's wish comes true. . . .*

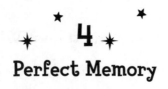

4

Perfect Memory

"I'm so glad your parents let you come with me," Izzy told Cassie and Alex as they climbed into the back of her mom's car.

"And we'll all be there to see you dance at the end of the class," Mrs. Nichols added.

Cassie and Alex were wearing shorts and T-shirts, but Izzy had on a leotard and tights. Her hair was pulled into a ponytail. "You look like a real ballerina," Cassie told her.

"Thanks," Izzy said. She smiled, but

Cassie noticed that she held her hands tightly together in her lap.

She's really worried, Cassie thought.

They drove down the hill and along the coast, where people were out enjoying the sunshine. Farther along the boardwalk, Cassie pointed out a reddish brown building with tall windows.

"That's the town hall. It's where the ballet class is being held," she said.

Mrs. Nichols parked in a space outside the town hall. As they all climbed out of the car, the other kids attending the class were walking up the wide stone steps that led into the building. Cassie, Alex, Izzy, and Mrs. Nichols followed.

"Move!" a girl screeched.

Cassie's heart sank. She looked around to see a familiar girl in a pink tutu and ballet shoes with ribbons wound around her ankles. The girl was spinning and twirling, knocking into everyone else.

"Who's that?" Izzy whispered.

"Donna Fox," Cassie replied. "Her parents own Flashley Manor, the biggest hotel in Astral-on-Sea."

"She always ruins everything," Alex muttered.

They headed through the doors and followed a sign that read *Ballet Class — This Way!* It directed them to a large hall with chairs around the edge, and an MP3 player and speakers on a table.

"Come in, dancers!" a tall man said.

He wore black pants and a white shirt. Stretching out his arms in welcome, he moved gracefully toward them.

"I'm Roman, your teacher," the man explained. "Now, let's all learn some ballet and have lots of fun. At the end of the class, we'll do a performance for all the moms and dads!"

"Doesn't that sound wonderful?" Mrs.

Nichols said. She waved good-bye. "See you later!"

Nearby, Donna fluffed up the frilly layers of her tutu. "I'm going to be the best dancer," she bragged. "I'm the best at everything."

The other kids were grinning excitedly, but Cassie noticed that Izzy was looking around nervously.

"First, we'll do some warm-up exercises," Roman said. He turned on the MP3 player, and the hall was filled with tinkling piano music. Roman lifted his arms up above his head. "Pretend you want to touch the stars," he said.

Cassie smiled. She knew what it felt like to touch a real star! All of the kids stretched their arms up, just like Roman showed them.

"Now swing your feet," Roman called.

As Cassie kicked her foot up, she saw Izzy swing her foot high in the air and back again.

"Very good!" Roman said, nodding to Izzy.

Izzy blushed.

When the warm-up was finished, Roman paused the music. "Excellent work," he said. "Now, if you've danced before, please come to the front of the class."

"Watch it," Donna snapped, pushing Izzy out of the way as she moved to the front of the room.

"I bet she's never danced in her life," Alex

said, scowling. "Remember her terrible performance at Lia's birthday party?"

Izzy moved close to Cassie and Alex, her hands shaking. "I think I'll stay with you," she said.

Roman looked over at Cassie, Alex, Izzy, and the other kids at the back. "You can learn a lot from watching other dancers," he told them. "Just have fun and relax. You'll pick it up in no time!"

Then Roman pressed the PLAY button on his MP3 player. Beautiful music floated through the air.

"Let's dance," he said. "First, gallop!"

Cassie, Alex, and Izzy all galloped around the room together. Alex neighed like a pony, making Izzy laugh.

"Now leap," Roman said. "And then pirouette—which means spin."

Together, they all leaped through the air and twirled around.

"Good job," Roman said. "You're all doing so well. Next, I want you to try an arabesque. That's a—"

Before Roman could explain, Izzy lifted her leg behind her and stretched out her arms. Cassie gasped. *She looks so elegant*, she thought.

"Look, everyone," Roman said. "That is a perfect arabesque."

Izzy blushed again.

"And now, let's do all the steps in order," Roman said.

This time, Cassie noticed that Izzy did a great gallop and leap, but forgot to spin before the arabesque.

"Not so perfect now, are you?" Donna sneered.

Poor Izzy tried again. But this time, she pirouetted at the wrong moment, bumping into Donna.

"Watch out, you clumsy girl!" Donna cried, glaring.

"I'm so s-sorry," Izzy stammered.

"Don't worry about Donna," Cassie whispered. But Izzy looked like she might cry.

I have to do something to make her wish come true, Cassie thought. *But what? I can't remember the routine, either. . . .*

Alex was repeating the steps quietly to himself. "Gallop, leap, turn, arabesque," he muttered.

Cassie was impressed. Even though Alex's leg pointed out in front for the arabesque

instead of behind, he was doing everything
in the right order.

Cassie whispered all the steps, too,
concentrating hard to memorize the routine.

Suddenly, she saw the heart charm glowing on her bracelet! Her own heart raced with excitement, and she ducked behind one of the floor-length curtains that hung from the windows so that no one would notice her.

A shower of glittering sparkles swirled around her bracelet and over her feet. Still hidden by the curtain, Cassie tried the dance steps again in order. Amazed, she found that now she could remember the routine perfectly!

Stella said that memories are precious, she thought, *and my heart charm gives me perfect memory. Now I know how to help Izzy!*

5

Cinderella's Dance

Cassie danced out from behind the curtain and through the class, until she was in front of Izzy and Alex.

"We're going to use my magic heart charm to help Izzy remember the steps," she told Alex quietly. Then she turned to Izzy and said, "Just follow my moves!"

Izzy watched Cassie carefully, then copied her sequence of steps. Cassie glanced over her shoulder and smiled. Her plan was working!

Izzy was dancing the routine perfectly. She looked great, leaping high, pointing her toes, and finally stretching her arms out in a graceful arabesque.

"Beautiful," Roman called out to Izzy.

She didn't blush this time. Her face beamed as she danced around the room, leaping, twirling, and holding the arabesque perfectly.

"She's got it!" Cassie said excitedly to Alex.

Alex turned to watch Izzy. "She sure does!" he agreed.

Cassie glanced down at her charm bracelet hopefully,

but her heart sank. She stopped dancing and
moved to the side of the room.

"What's wrong?" Alex asked, following her.

"I thought I made Izzy's wish come true
and earned my last charm," Cassie
said. "But it hasn't appeared."

She and Alex looked at
each other. What had gone
wrong?

Roman clapped his
hands. The class all
came to a halt—except
for Donna, who spun right
into Roman.

"Be careful of those
around you," Roman told
her. "This isn't a solo dance."

With that, Donna stomped off to the other side of the room and sulked.

Now that class was almost over, their audience started to arrive! The seats around the edge of the room were soon packed. Cassie and Alex spotted their parents, and Izzy waved excitedly to her mom.

"Are you okay?" Cassie asked her.

"I'm fine now," Izzy replied with a smile as she practiced her arabesque again. "I managed to dance that new routine in front of a whole class of strangers, thanks to you. I've never had so much fun dancing before, because I'm always too worried about remembering the steps. You two are magical!"

Roman clapped his hands again, and the kids all lined up. As the music began, Izzy galloped confidently across the room, with Cassie and Alex dancing along beside her. When they got to the arabesque, Izzy's foot stretched high in the air.

Cassie noticed that Izzy had been dancing so freely that her hair had come loose and whirled around her, just like it had in the observatory that morning. She looked so happy! Cassie smiled. She had definitely granted Izzy's wish. So why hadn't she received her final charm?

The audience clapped as the dance came

to an end. Suddenly, some new music came
on the MP3 player. Roman had accidentally
tapped the wrong button.

"Oops," he said, moving to turn it off.

But Izzy kept on dancing to the new music,
her feet spinning across the floor. Cassie

recognized the jumps and arm movements from Izzy's dance in the observatory.

"I think that's her *Cinderella* routine," she said to Alex. "And look—she's not nervous at all."

Izzy dipped and leaped, finishing with a pirouette, spinning on the spot so her hair flew out around her.

When she finished the dance, everyone except Donna applauded loudly. Izzy glowed.

"I didn't worry about the steps. They just came naturally," Izzy told Cassie and Alex in excitement. "I was enjoying dancing too much."

Izzy's mom walked over and joined them. She was beaming. "That was fantastic! I'm so proud of you," she said, hugging Izzy.

"She dances from her heart," Roman said, walking up to the group. "Izzy, the audience will always love you when you dance with such joy."

"I can't wait to perform *Cinderella*, now that I know I can remember the steps," said Izzy. "And it's all thanks to both of you!" She smiled at Cassie and Alex.

Cassie smiled back, but inside she couldn't help feeling disappointed. On her wrist, her bracelet tingled in a strange way, but her final charm still hadn't appeared.

I wonder why, she thought. *Without my next charm, how will I ever become a Lucky Star?*

6

A New Lucky Star

With a heavy heart, Cassie stood in the hallway of Starwatcher Towers. The afternoon at the beach was over and Izzy had gone out with her mom, leaving Cassie and Alex to say good-bye.

Outside, Cassie could hear her mom and dad talking to Alex's parents.

"We've had such a wonderful time," Alex's dad was saying. "Astral-on-Sea is so much more peaceful than our busy city. We'll stop at the pier on the way home and enjoy the view for the last time."

"Yes, this is a very relaxing place," Alex's mom agreed. "I think we all wish we lived here!"

I wish you did, too, thought Cassie. She glanced at Alex. His suitcase stood next to him, with the photo album Cassie had given him balanced on top. He took his glasses off and polished them on his sleeve.

"I'm sorry you didn't get your final charm," he said sadly. "Then you could make my mom's wish come true."

"At least we granted Izzy's wish," Cassie replied.

Alex nodded and cleared his throat, popping his glasses back on. "I can't seem to

stop my glasses from fogging up," he said.

Cassie knew Alex was trying not to cry. She felt the same way.

"I'll miss you," she said.

Alex nodded. "I'll miss you, too."

Placing a paw on Cassie's knee, Comet gave a little whine. *"MEOW!"*

Cassie and Alex jumped as Twinkle ran into the hallway, meowing loudly.

"He came out of the shed!" Cassie said, stroking Twinkle's fluffy fur. "I think he wants to say good-bye to Comet."

She concentrated on her crescent moon charm. Silver sparkles swirled around her bracelet, and sprinkled over Twinkle and Comet.

"Comet likes that towel, so I want to give it to him to remember me by," Twinkle meowed.

"That's awfully nice of you, Twinkle," Cassie said.

Comet ran over to Twinkle and licked his ears.

"Thank you, thank you," he barked.

"Okay, okay," Twinkle grumbled, but Cassie could see that he was pleased. "It's been very interesting to have a puppy friend. Now, I have to get back to my pile of sacks."

Cassie translated for Alex.

"There are lots of scientific theories about friendship," Alex said after a pause. "You and I will be friends forever — that's my prediction."

"We'll see each other again, I just know it," Cassie whispered, hugging him.

"Good-bye for now," Alex said, squeezing her extra-hard.

"Time to go!" Alex's mom called.

Trying not to cry, Cassie followed Alex outside.

Alex and Comet got into the car, Alex clutching his photo album the whole time. Comet sat on the towel. Cassie stood next to her parents, waving as they drove away slowly.

A tear slid down Cassie's cheek. She pulled one of her pretty star-dotted tissues from her pocket and wiped her eyes.

Cassie's dad patted her shoulder gently.

"It's hard to say good-bye, isn't it?" her mom said. "Come on, let's go inside."

"I'd like to stay out here for a little while," Cassie replied.

"Okay," her mom said, kissing the top of Cassie's head on her way into the house. "Come in whenever you're ready."

Cassie sat down on the doorstep. It was such a sad day: Twinkle hiding in the shed, Alex going home, and no sign of her last charm.

But at least I have lots of good memories, she

thought, peering at her heart-shaped charm.

She looked up at the evening sky. It was full of dark clouds without a star in sight. Except . . .

Cassie jumped up, her heart lifting. A brilliant orb of light was heading toward Starwatcher Towers, aiming straight for the curved roof of her bedroom.

She ran into the house. Her mom and dad looked up in surprise as she rushed past them.

"Cassie?" her dad asked. "Are you all right?"

"Just going upstairs," she called. "There's something I have to do!"

Cassie raced up to her bedroom and pulled the lever that opened the glass panel of her ceiling. *Whoosh!* The orb spun into the room.

With a *whizz* and a *fizz* and a *zip-zip-zip*, the orb slowly changed into Stella Starkeeper! Cassie gasped. Wearing a new silver dress, with a long, flowing skirt and a bodice covered in sparkling jewels, Stella looked even more magical than ever.

Stella raised her wand and filled the bedroom with tiny glittering stars.

"I am so proud of you, Cassie," she said, kissing Cassie on the cheek.

"But I've let you down," Cassie said sadly. She held the pretty bracelet up for Stella to see. "I didn't earn my last charm."

"Oh, but you did," Stella explained. "You helped Izzy's wish come true, didn't you? It's just that this charm is so special, I wanted to give it to you myself."

Stella unclipped a star-shaped charm from the bracelet on her own wrist and attached it to Cassie's. It was just like the star on the top of Stella's wand.

Stella touched the new charm with her wand, and a shower of tiny glittering stars fluttered over Cassie.

She felt like jumping up and down with joy. She had done it, after all! But then she glanced at Alex's shining crystals and remembered that he wasn't here to share the excitement.

I'll have to write and tell him, she thought sadly.

"Congratulations, Cassie," said Stella. "You've always watched and listened for someone to make a wish — someone who really deserved your help. And now that you're a Lucky Star, you can grant wishes anytime." She smiled. "Now it's your turn to make three wishes."

What will I wish for? Cassie thought, looking up at the cloudy night sky. And then she realized. *I know just what my first wish will be. . . .*

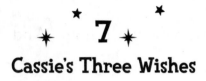

7

Cassie's Three Wishes

Whoosh!

Hand in hand, Stella and Cassie flew through the open window of Cassie's bedroom. Light as balloons, they circled over Starwatcher Towers. In the observatory, Cassie could see her dad shaking his head sadly.

"What will your first wish be?" Stella asked.

"Today is my mom and dad's wedding

anniversary. Dad was really excited because there's supposed to be a meteor shower tonight," Cassie explained. "But it's too cloudy to see it. As a special gift, I'd like to make their anniversary absolutely perfect."

"Make your wish," Stella said.

Cassie thought hard about her star-shaped charm.

"I wish the dark clouds would go away," she said.

Silvery stardust swirled from the charm, out across the night sky. The dark clouds scudded away.

Delighted, Cassie watched her dad's face break into a grin as her mom walked into the observatory. Cassie's dad pointed up at the glorious night sky, twinkling with starlight.

Cassie and Stella flew quickly into the backyard, so they wouldn't be seen.

Then Cassie spotted Twinkle through the shed window, sitting sadly on the pile of sacks. "I know what my second wish is!" she said with a grin.

Cassie thought hard about her star-shaped charm again. "I wish Twinkle would understand how much we love him," she said.

Silvery stardust swirled around her bracelet and over the yard. A trail of Twinkle's favorite treats appeared, leading out of the shed and into Starwatcher Towers.

Happily munching, Twinkle followed the treats all the way to Cassie's room. Cassie and Stella flew from window to window, watching him go.

★　✳　★　✳

"Look!" Cassie said to Stella as they gazed down through the glass ceiling. "Twinkle has a brand-new cat basket with his name written on it."

"And there are gorgeous, soft blankets inside," Stella said.

Cassie thought hard about her crescent moon charm. Sparkles swirled over her wrist and through the open window to Twinkle.

"I hope you like your new basket, Twinkle," Cassie said. "I wanted to give you a gift that's a spot of your very own!"

"I love it," Twinkle purred, settling down on the blankets. "And I love you, Cassie!"

Cassie giggled and blew Twinkle a kiss.

"You have one more wish left," Stella said.

Cassie knew exactly what she was going to wish for.

It's a very big wish, she thought nervously. *I wonder if it's too big. . . .*

She led Stella up into the sky, high above the boardwalk and along the beach, where the waves were moving in and out with the tide. They flew over the theater and the town hall, above Flashley Manor Hotel and the Fairy Cupcake Bakery. Finally, they stopped at the pier. Alex's car was driving away, leaving Astral-on-Sea behind.

Cassie flew quickly, following the road out of the town.

Will my wish work? she wondered. *That would be the most magical gift of all. . . .*

Cassie concentrated really hard on her star-shaped charm. She remembered that Alex's mom had wished that they all lived in Astral-on-Sea. Most of all, she thought about Alex, and how he'd become her best friend.

"I wish Alex and his mom and dad lived in Astral-on-Sea," she said.

The silver sparkles swirled around her bracelet, then showered the roof of the car. Cassie held her breath.

The car slowed down and pulled over. Cassie's heart beat faster. She and Stella flew closer and hid behind a hedge so they wouldn't be seen. Through the car window, Cassie could see Alex leaning forward to listen to his parents.

"I don't want to leave this beautiful town," his mom was saying.

"Neither do I," his dad agreed. "I could stay here forever."

"Let's live at Starwatcher Towers!" Alex piped up from the backseat.

"We can't live at a B&B, sweetheart," his mom said.

Outside, Cassie watched nervously. Would they drive away?

Alex's dad looked first at Alex's mom, and then at Alex.

"Are we all sure this is where we want to live?" he asked.

"Yes, yes, yes! Please," Alex begged. His mom nodded. "I can't think of anywhere else I'd rather be," she said. "That settles it," his dad said, smiling. "We'll stay at Starwatcher Towers until we find a place of our own in Astral-on-Sea."

Cassie's heart soared. Her wish had been granted. This was the most wonderful day ever!

Once Alex's dad had turned the car around to head back to town, Cassie and Stella flew home. They dropped gently through the open panel into Cassie's bedroom. Twinkle meowed softly from his new bed.

Cassie put her arms around Stella and gave her a huge hug.

"Thank you for helping me become a Lucky Star," she said.

"It was all your hard work, Cassie," Stella replied. "And now that you're a Lucky Star, you'll be able to help many more people."

With a wink and a shower of sparkles, Stella disappeared.

All seven magical charms tinkled together on Cassie's wrist.

I wonder whose wish I'll grant next, Cassie thought.

"There you are, darling," said her mom, poking her head into Cassie's bedroom. "Dad and I are going outside to watch the meteor shower. Do you want to come?"

"Yes, please," Cassie said, her eyes shining. She pulled on her coat and ran downstairs.

Cassie stood between her mom and dad. Overhead, the first meteors streaked silvery trails across the night sky.

"Magical," breathed Cassie.

In the distance, a car's headlights appeared,

weaving up the road toward the B&B.

"That looks like Alex's car," her dad said. "They're coming back!"

Cassie gave a whoop of excitement. She couldn't wait to show Alex her new charm.

High above, one special star shone extra brightly. "See you soon, Stella, and thanks again," Cassie murmured. "I wonder what my next adventure will be."

Make Your Own!

Cassie knows all about being a good friend! She even makes Alex a great photo album, so they can remember their time together. A friendship scrapbook is a perfect gift for your best friend!

You Need:
- An album with paper pages
- Double-sided tape or glue
- Photos, ticket stubs, notes, and other mementos that remind you of your friend
- Markers or sparkly pens

1. Organize the different photos and mementos in whatever order you like. You can arrange them by date, theme, or put them in a random order!
2. Use double-sided tape or glue to stick the photos and mementos to each page of the album.
3. Write fun captions or quotes on the pages, using markers or sparkly pens. These can be funny jokes or sweet memories that you and your friend share!
4. Personalize the front cover of the album with markers or sparkly pens, if you like.

Now you have a fun friendship scrapbook to share with your very best friend!

KITTY CORNER

Where kitties get the love they need

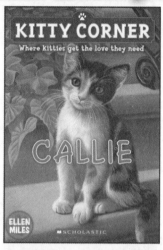

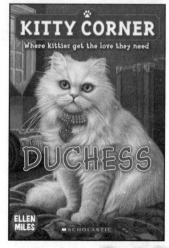

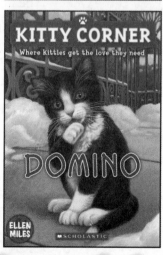

These purr-fect kittens need a home!

There's Magic in Every Series!

The Rainbow Fairies
The Weather Fairies
The Jewel Fairies
The Pet Fairies
The Fun Day Fairies
The Petal Fairies
The Dance Fairies
The Music Fairies
The Sports Fairies
The Party Fairies
The Ocean Fairies
The Night Fairies
The Magical Animal Fairies
The Princess Fairies

Read them all!

■SCHOLASTIC

www.scholastic.com
www.rainbowmagiconline.com

HIT entertainment

RMFAIR®